Friend Dog

Friend Dog

by ROBERT WAHL
illustrated by JOE EWERS

Little, Brown and Company

Boston · Toronto

First Edition

Library of Congress Cataloging-in-Publication Data

Wahl, Robert, 1948–
Friend dog/by Robert Wahl ; illustrated by Joe Ewers. — 1st ed.
p. cm.
Summary: A toddler and the family's new puppy play hard the day
Mother brings Friend Dog home.
ISBN 0-316-91710-9
[1. Dogs — Fiction. 2. Babies — Fiction. 3. Stories in rhyme.]
I. Ewers, Joe, ill. II. Title.
PZ8.3.W134Fr   1988
[E] — dc19   87-25069
                                         CIP
                                         AC

10 9 8 7 6 5 4 3 2 1

NIL

Published simultaneously in Canada
by Little, Brown & Company (Canada) Limited

Printed in Italy

For Nina Marie

R. W.

To my kids, Chris, Erik, and Kim,
and Lady, their dog

J. E.

Baby in the playpen,
Baby all alone,

Until one day
Mother brought Dog home.

Four legs, two legs —
one fast, one slow.

Baby sat; Dog zzzipped!
Go, Dog, go!

Running and jumping,
lickety-*lickety-split!*

Baby kept on spinning
'til Dog finally quit.

Into the kitchen
and out the back door,

Dog started digging,
then dug some more.

When Baby got a cookie,
what did he do?

Umm-humm...

Dog liked cookies,
so he dug that one up, too.

Then Baby crept over
and stole Dog's bone.

"No, no!" cried Mother.
"Leave that *icky* thing alone!"

Back in the house,
Dog scurried to his plate.

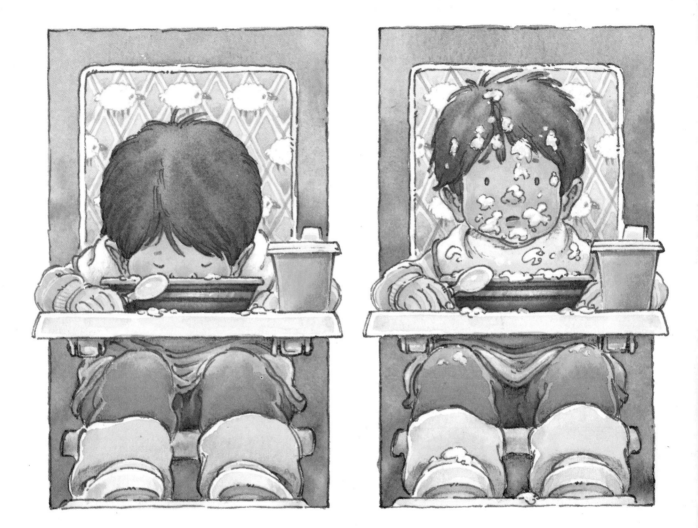

Baby did what Dog did
and ate and ate and ate.

Into the living room,
back on the floor,

What did they get into?
A great tug-of-war!

The two tugged away,
so long and so fast

'til upstairs they went,
tired out at last.

Water in the bath —
rub-a-dub-dub.

Look out, soap!
There're two in the tub.

Then sleepy, clean,
and happily fed,

one into his basket
and one into his bed.

"Good night," said Mother.
"Your day is at an end.

Sleep tight, Baby,
and your new best friend!"

Friend Dog.